Dear Family and Friends of Young Readers,

Learning to read is one of the most important milestones your child will ever attain. Early reading is hard work, but you can make it easier with Hello Readers.

Just like learning to play a sport or an instrument, learning to read requires many opportunities to work on skills. However, you have to get in the game or experience real music to keep interested and motivated. Hello Readers are carefully structured to provide the right level of text for practice and great stories for experiencing the fun of reading.

Try these activities:

• Reading starts with the alphabet and at the earliest level, you may encourage your child to focus on the sounds of letters in words and sounding out words. With more experienced readers, focus on how words are spelled. Be word watchers!

• Go beyond the book — talk about the story, how it compares with other stories, and what your child likes about it.

• Comprehension — did your child get it? Have your child retell the story or answer questions you may ask about it.

Another thing children learn to do at this age is learn to ride a bike. You put training wheels on to help them in the beginning and guide the bike from behind. Hello Readers help you support your child and then you get to watch them take off as skilled readers.

— Francie Alexander
   Chief Academic Officer,
   Scholastic Education

For Papa George, the best storyteller of all.
—M.S.

ISBN 0-439-44154-4

Text copyright © 2003 by Marilyn Snyder.
Illustrations copyright © 2003 by Lena Shiffman.
All rights reserved. Published by Scholastic Inc. SCHOLASTIC, HELLO READER!, and associated logos are trademarks and/or registered trademarks of Scholastic Inc.

12 11 10 9 8 7 6 5 4 3 2 1   3 4 5 6 7 8/0

Printed in the U.S.A.
First printing, March 2003

A Second Chance for Tina

by **Marilyn Snyder**
Illustrated by **Lena Shiffman**

Hello Reader! — Level 3

SCHOLASTIC INC.
New York Toronto London Auckland Sydney
Mexico City New Delhi Hong Kong Buenos Aires

This is the story of how a little girl
named Rebecca helped to save a
big elephant named Tina.

When Rebecca was eight years old, she lived
in New York City with her family.
Every Wednesday after school, Rebecca and her
Grandpa Arthur visited the Central Park Zoo.

It was one of Rebecca's favorite
things to do.
And her favorite animal in the zoo
was an Asian elephant named Tina.

Tina always waved her trunk when
she saw Rebecca.
The little girl always fed her peanuts.
Tina's keeper was a man named Bob.
He let Rebecca give Tina a pail of raw beets,
the elephant's favorite snack.
Rebecca learned all about Tina from Bob.
He told her that Tina had come to the zoo
from Asia when she was five years old.

She had been put in a cage with a
much larger and older elephant named Julia.
But Julia had died a short time ago.
Tina was very sad without Julia.
"I'm the only friend she has now,"
Bob told Rebecca, "except, of course,
when you come to visit."

When Rebecca and Grandpa Arthur came
on their next visit, Bob was not there.
Tina was in the corner of her cage.
She wouldn't come over to the bars
to say hello.
Something was very wrong.
Grandpa Arthur asked one of the other
keepers where he could find Bob.
"I'm so sorry," said the keeper,
"but I have some sad news about Bob.
He suddenly became very ill and died.
We all miss him a great deal."
Rebecca and Grandpa Arthur were very,
very unhappy.
Bob had been so kind to them and to Tina.

"Who will take care of Tina now?"
Rebecca asked.

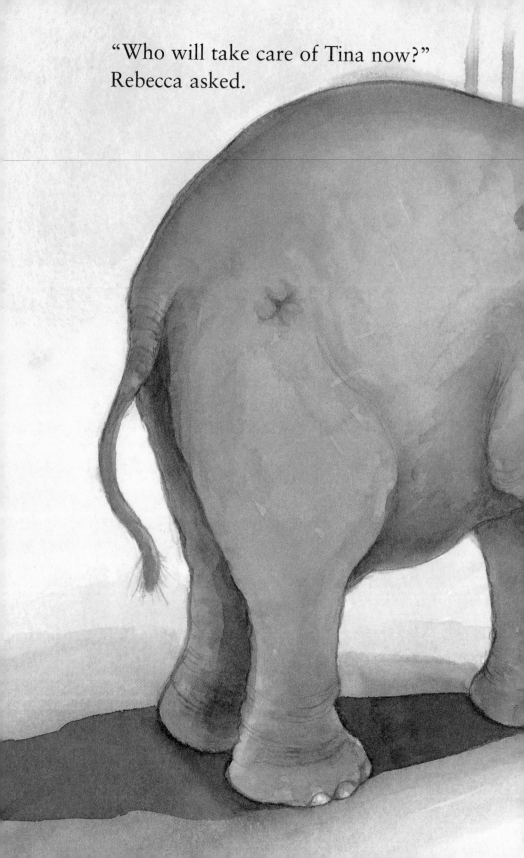

"Well," the keeper said sadly, "that's a big problem. Tina is so unhappy about losing both Julia and Bob that she won't let anyone else near her. Last week, she tried to crush the arm of one keeper. Then she stepped on the foot of another. And they were only trying to feed her! Now we have to push her food through the cage door."

Rebecca was very upset.
"What will happen to her?" she asked.
"I honestly don't know," the keeper said.
"You see, the zoo is closing soon. A better
zoo will be built in its place. That means
that all of the animals have to be placed
in other zoos for now. Everyone has been
adopted so far, except Tina. Zookeepers
from all over the world have come to see her.
But they won't take her when they see
how angry she is."

"Oh, no," said Rebecca. "What happens if no one takes her?"

The keeper said that Tina would have to be destroyed if no one could be found to save her. Rebecca and Grandpa Arthur walked sadly to Tina's cage.

Tears were on Rebecca's cheeks as she held up a handful of peanuts for Tina to see.

After a few minutes, Tina seemed to recognize her old friends and slowly lumbered over to the cage bars.

She took the peanuts and offered her trunk for Rebecca to stroke.

"You see, Grandpa, she still knows us. She knows we love her," said Rebecca, blinking back tears.

"Too bad we don't have room for an elephant at home," said Grandpa Arthur, trying to make Rebecca smile.

That night, Rebecca lay awake worrying.
She had to do something to help!
But she was only eight years old.
Who would listen to her?

Early the next morning, the phone rang.
It was Grandpa Arthur.
"Sweetheart," he said, "I have an idea about Tina.
Why not write to people who can help save her?
We can send letters to the zoo, the newspaper,
and the mayor. What do you think?"
Rebecca was excited.
Just the thought of doing something to help
took some of the sadness away.
It made her feel grown-up and useful.

That afternoon, Rebecca and Grandpa Arthur
wrote their letters.

They wrote to *The New York Times*, the
mayor of New York City, the commissioner
of parks, and the Zoological Society.
Rebecca sealed the envelopes and licked
the stamps.

Grandpa Arthur held the mailbox slot open as
she slid the envelopes inside and made a wish.

One week went by.
Then Grandpa Arthur called Rebecca.
"Guess what, honey. *The New York Times*
printed your letter this morning!"
There it was in black and white!
Rebecca was so excited she could hardly
sit still in school that day.
Her teacher, Ms. Eldredge, posted the letter
on the bulletin board.

During the next few days, letters came to Rebecca
from the mayor, the parks commissioner, and the
Zoological Society.
They all promised to help.
Now I'm not the only one who cares, Rebecca
thought. *At least that's something!*
But time was running out.

The zoo was going to close in two weeks,
and still no one had offered to take Tina.
Rebecca was so worried she couldn't think
about anything else.
She even missed three easy words on her
spelling test.
Then, on their next visit, Rebecca and
Grandpa Arthur were surprised to see
a stranger in Tina's cage.
And he was feeding her raw beets!
Best of all, Tina was letting him stroke
her trunk.

Rebecca and Grandpa Arthur watched while Tina finished the last of her snack. The stranger gave her trunk a final pat. He picked up the empty food pail and came out of the cage.

"You must be Rebecca," he said, holding out his hand and smiling. "I've heard a lot about you. It's a pleasure to meet a fellow elephant lover."

Rebecca thought he had the nicest smile she'd ever seen.

No wonder Tina trusted him!

His name was David Blasko, but he said most people called him Dave.

He worked at Six Flags/Marine World in California.

Dave told Rebecca and Grandpa Arthur that he had read their letter in *The New York Times*.

He had arrived at the Central Park Zoo several days earlier.

Dave had spent the first few days gently talking to Tina and feeding her treats from outside her cage.

At first, Tina refused to come out
of her corner.
Then, slowly, she began to trust him
and take the treats he offered.

Finally, that very morning, Dave decided
to enter the cage.
He knew he could help Tina if she did
not attack him.
"I think she's just very lonely," he said.
"After all, she's lost her two closest friends:
her cage mate and her keeper."
At last, thought Rebecca, *someone
who really understands elephants!
Especially Tina!*

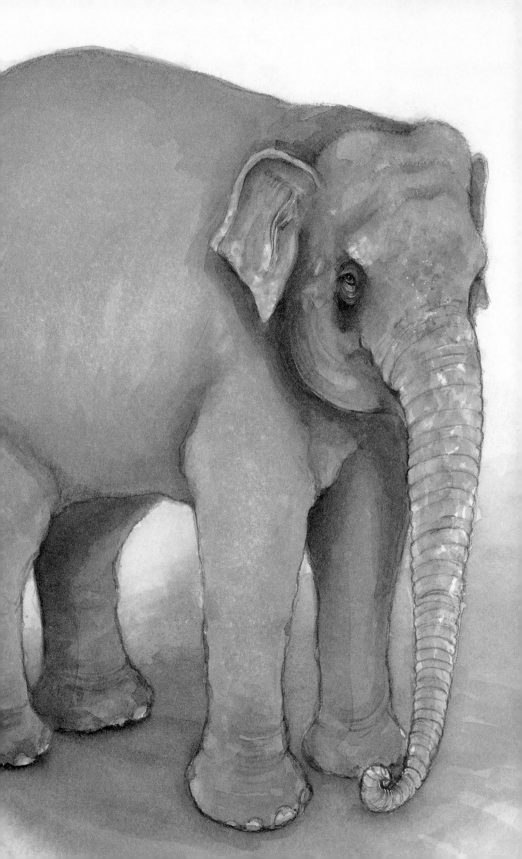

Tina did let Dave into the cage, which
was a big relief to everyone.
"What happens now?" Rebecca
asked excitedly.
"Now we take Tina out to her new home
in California," said Dave. "We'll drive her
across the country in a special van."
He winked at Rebecca and Grandpa Arthur.
"Would you like to come?"
Rebecca looked up at Grandpa Arthur.
"Oh, could we?" she whispered.
"I don't know, honey," he replied. "Aren't
you forgetting something important?
Like school?"
"But next week is spring vacation, Grandpa.
We could fly home in time for school again.
Oh, pretty please!" she pleaded, jumping
up and down.

Grandpa Arthur thought for a moment.
"Well, I guess you could say that this trip
will be a good life lesson. Sure, we'll go!"
They would leave the following Monday.
It would take several days to drive all the
way across the country.
Rebecca was so excited the night before
the trip that she could hardly sleep.

She and Grandpa Arthur arrived at the
zoo at six o'clock on Monday morning.
They saw a huge van backed up to Tina's
cage door.
A ramp was lowered so that she could be
led into the van.

Rebecca was surprised to see
a crowd of people waiting nearby.
She recognized the other keepers
and the parks commissioner.
There was also a reporter and a
photographer from *The New York Times*.
Dave introduced Rebecca and
Grandpa Arthur to his boss, Peter, who
had come from California to help.
They also met Frank, the driver of the van,
and another trainer named Jim.

But the biggest surprise of all was Rebecca's
teacher, Ms. Eldredge, and her entire
third-grade class.
They had come to see Rebecca and Tina off
on their big adventure!

The commissioner walked over to Rebecca. "So, this is the famous letter writer," he said, smiling and shaking her hand. "You are really something, young lady. Without your hard work, we might have never found a new home for Tina."

Rebecca blushed, and Grandpa Arthur smiled proudly.

Dave explained to the group that Tina had been
given medicine to make her calm and sleepy.
This would help them lead her easily into the van.
After all, he told them, Tina had not been out of
her cage in many years.
Dave didn't want to frighten her.

Everything was ready.
Dave opened the cage door and started
to lead Tina up the ramp.
Rebecca crossed her fingers and held
her breath.
Suddenly, halfway up the ramp, Tina
yawned, sat down with a big thud,
and fell asleep!
The keepers could not move her.
What do you do when an elephant
falls asleep?

Rebecca discovered that you just wait until she
decides to wake up!
She and Grandpa Arthur sat down on a bench
to wait and listen to Tina snore.
Ms. Eldredge and the class left the park.
The commissioner had to go back to his office
and the zookeepers had to take care of the
other animals.
Rebecca and Grandpa Arthur waited.
And waited.
And waited.
They even napped a little, too.

Then, just when they were beginning
to wonder if Tina would ever wake up,
she opened her eyes.
She yawned an elephant-size yawn
and slowly got to her feet.
Dave led her the rest of the way into
the van, and he and Jim put her safely
in place.
Frank climbed into the driver's seat
with Rebecca beside him.
Grandpa Arthur, Dave, and Jim rode
in the back to watch Tina and keep
her company.
They all waved good-bye and slowly
drove away.

The trip went smoothly, even through
a snowstorm in the Dakotas.

The grown-ups took turns reading
the map and caring for Tina.
Finally, they reached
Six Flags/Marine World.

It was a beautiful, sunny
California morning.
Dave had phoned ahead to tell his
keepers that Tina would be arriving.
He had asked them to line up the park's
ten other elephants to greet Tina when
she arrived.
Rebecca was happy to hear that Tina
would not be living in a cage.
The elephant's new home was a
wonderful jungle area, much like
her own native country.

Dave explained to Rebecca and Grandpa
Arthur that elephants are friendly animals.
The company of other elephants is very
important to them.
But Dave was worried because Tina had
been alone for so long.

Would she know that the other elephants were her friends, or would they only frighten her?

Everyone waited nervously as the van's ramp was lowered.

The waiting elephants took one look at Tina in the van, raised their trunks, and trumpeted a very loud welcome.

A good beginning indeed!

Now it was Tina's turn.
It was so quiet you could hear a pin drop.
The seconds ticked slowly by.
Finally, Tina lifted her trunk and
trumpeted back.

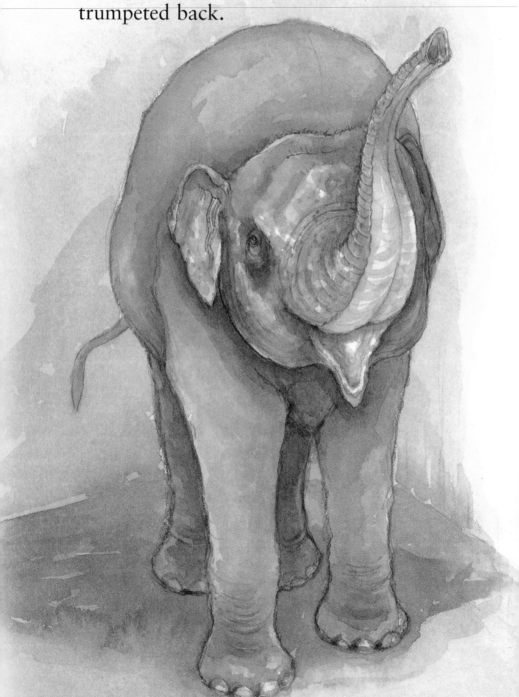

Everyone cheered!
Rebecca and Grandpa Arthur hugged each
other, and then they both hugged Dave.
They had taken a chance and it had worked!
Tina had a new home and new friends.
She had been given a second chance at life!

It was a very happy ending for what could have been a very sad story. "It just goes to show, Grandpa," said Rebecca, "you should never give up hope. Even if you're an elephant."